Bennie Goes Up! Up! Up!

written by
Joy Eastridge & Brynn Welch

illustrated by
Mary Ruth Pruitt

For Benjamin Graham, my best luck.

-BW

To my grandchildren, Olivia, Owen, and Malia.
May you grow Up! Up! Up! and bring others with you.

-JE

Bennie reaches up, up, up.
He sees the stars.

Bennie loves soaring up, up, up high.

Bennie crawls up, up, up the stairs.
His mom helps him sometimes.

Bennie climbs
up, up, up the ladder.
He loves to slide down
and climb back up.

Bennie rides up, up, up the escalator.
He keeps his feet still and feels
himself move all the way up to the top.

Bennie pushes the button
and zooms up the elevator.
The elevator goes fast:
up, up, up!

Bennie flies up, up, up in the helicopter.
It swoops around town.

Bennie scales the mountain.
He goes up, up, up
one step at a time
until he gets to the peak.

Bennie looks up, up, up.

He sees a bird fly by. He wants to fly too!

Bennie floats up, up, up
into the blue sky
and toward the pink cirrus clouds.

Bennie glides up, up, up through the troposphere.
The glider swooshes along, fast and quiet.

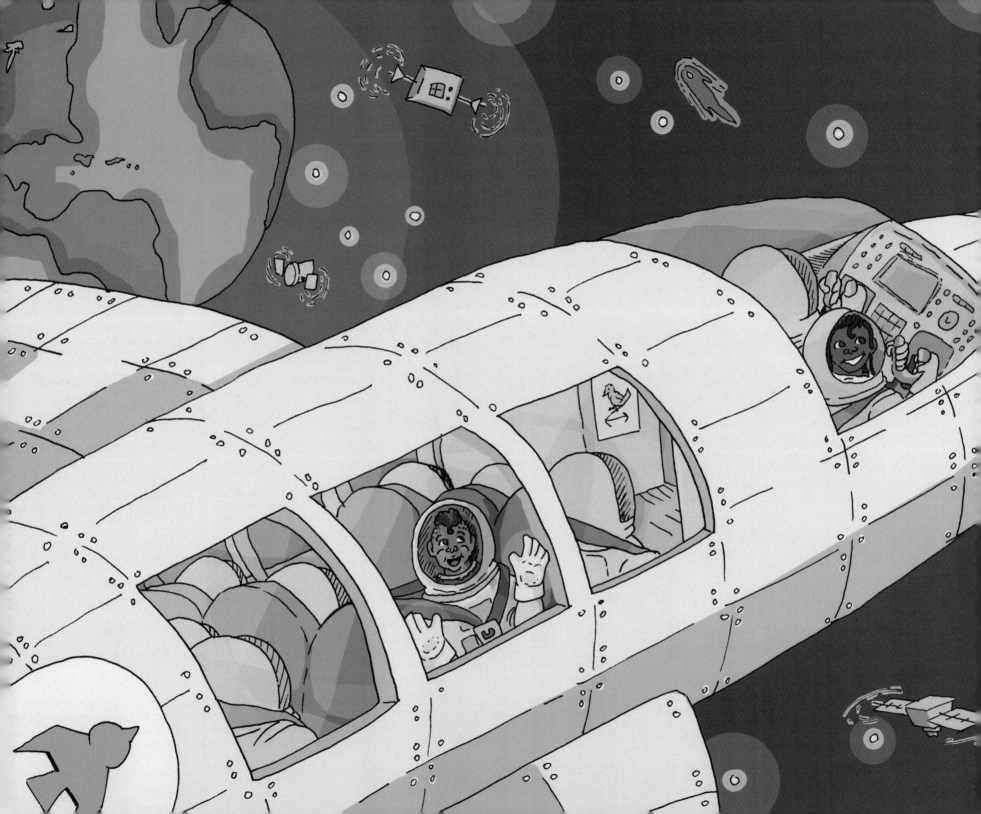

Bennie booms up, up, up
through the stratosphere.
He visits the International Space Station.

Bennie blasts up, up, up
through the mesosphere into outer space.

Bennie dreams.
In his dreams he invents
ways to go up, up, up.
Where do you
think he will go?

Where do you think
Bennie will go next?
Visit
upupup.world
to tell us!

Dr. Brynn Welch teaches philosophy at the University of Alabama at Birmingham. A long-time lover of children's books, she wants all children to be able to see themselves in the ordinary and extraordinary worlds those pages contain. *Bennie Goes Up! Up! Up!* is her first children's book, inspired by her son's sweet smile and his fascination with elevators.

Joy Eastridge, RN, works as a Faith Community Nurse in her local congregation. She enjoys writing Bible studies and is a regular contributor to a nursing website. She loves working toward making the world a better place for children to grow up.

Mary Ruth Pruitt is an educator and illustrator presently working in Memphis, Tennessee. She was brought up with a deep appreciation for storytelling and developed a passion for bringing narratives to life through her art. *Bennie Goes Up! Up! Up!* is her first children's book and represents a year of work and a lifetime of dreams.

CPSIA information can be obtained at www.ICGtesting.com
Printed in the USA
BVIW12n0536240318
511392BV00004B/7